LIFE ON MARS: THE REALITY OF LIVING ON THE RED PLANET

COPYRIGHT

Cover designed by Getcovers
Illustrations by TJ
1 edition 2024

ISBN 978-82-693890-2-9

WELCOME TO MARS, WHERE EVERYTHING IS ALMOST NORMAL

Congratulations! You've made it to Mars—humanity's bold new frontier where daily life has a few...twists. Need a coffee? Expect it to taste like freeze-dried sadness. Thinking of jogging? Prepare to float rather than run. Life here is like Earth, but with extra red dust and fewer functional gadgets. Yet somehow, amidst the chaos, It has a charm. It's not perfect, but hey, neither was Earth. Adjust your oxygen settings and settle in—living on Mars is just starting to get interesting.

Climb on board

BETSY
2050

RED DUST AND NEW BEGINNINGS

Sara Thompson wasn't your average space nerd. Sure, she had a collection of Star Trek mugs and could recite pi to fifty digits (a party trick that never got her any dates), but she was just a regular engineer who happened to hate Earth traffic enough to move to Mars.

At 32, she'd been crushing it in Silicon Valley, where her biggest challenges were deciding which overpriced food truck to hit for lunch and explaining to her mom why she was still single. Then came the email that changed everything: "Congratulations! You've been selected for Mars colonization!" She almost marked it as spam.

Five years later, Sara's traded her designer coffee for recycled water and her cushy coding job for the totally-not-stressful position of "Please Don't Let Everyone Suffocate" Manager (officially known as Martian Oxygen Distribution Manager, but that doesn't capture the daily panic).
Her apartment on Mars? Think college dorm meets space station, with the added charm of red dust that gets EVERYWHERE. Seriously, she's found it in places that defy physics. Her engineering degree comes in handy for figuring out how to stop her toilet from floating away during gravity fluctuations.

Living next door is Dan, the human equivalent of a golden

retriever in a spacesuit. While Sara's busy calculating how many ways things could go wrong, Dan's trying to start a Martian volleyball league or planning movie nights where every film is, space-related.

The job's not what she imagined when she watched sci-fi as a kid. Instead of making first contact with aliens, she made first contact with bizarre machinery errors and filing reports about oxygen consumption rates. Her main achievements include preventing three major oxygen disasters and winning the colony's first (and last) minimal-gravity ping pong tournament, which ended with two broken monitors and a new safety protocol.

But hey, at least she's got a killer view of the red planet - when she's not cursing at it during dust storms or trying to grow tomatoes that don't taste like metal. Plus, she's the only one from her graduating class who can say, "Sorry, I can't make the reunion—I'm on another world"
Welcome to Sara's life on Mars: where every day is a adventure in not dying, and the coffee situation is officially as a crisis.

WELCOME TO YOUR NEW HOME - MARS!

Sara's morning started like any other: with coffee that tasted like someone had filtered rocket fuel through an old sock. She stared out her window at the same old red landscape, as if a gigantic bottle of ketchup had been spilled across the horizon.

"What's up, Mars? Ready to try killing us in creativ and exciting ways today?" she mumbled into her cup.

BING! Her comm panel lit up:

DAILY ANNOUNCEMENT:
> Today's oxygen comes with a surprise lavender scent!
> Think of it as a free aromatherapy session.
> Side effects may include speaking in a higher pitch and spontaneous poetry recitation.
> Have a breathtaking day!
"Fantastic," Sara groaned. "Now my oxygen's getting fancy."

Her hover-bike, Betsy, was in the shop ("No, ma'am, "fix-it spray" doesn't get the job done in space"), which meant taking the public hover-bus. Joy. At least she'd get to watch her fellow Martians attempt the circus act of "trying to eat breakfast while floating."

Outside her apartment, her neighbor Dan was doing his usual morning routine: hoping to grow hair using Mars's radiation. He resembled a hopeful egg dressed in a spacesuit.

"Beautiful morning, Sara!" Dan shouted, waving while tying down his collection of garden gnomes (all named Neil Armstrong).

"Sure, Dan. Nothing says 'beautiful' like toxic dust and the constant threat of explosive decompression."

At the transport hub, Sara witnessed the entertainment: a couple arguing about solar panel cleaning duty."I cleaned them last dust storm!" "That was two months ago!" "Time works different on Mars!"

The hover-bus ride was its own adventure. Sara dodged three floating sandwiches, one rogue coffee cup, and what she hoped was just someone's escaped breakfast burrito.

The guy next to her was reading "Mars for Dummies: Because Earth Was Too Easy."

Looking out at the Mars colonies—A cluster of domes that seemed as if someone had scattered spacecraft parts like marbles—Sara couldn't help but smile. Sure, their vegetables tasted like regret, their wine was just sad algae juice, and their oxygen sometimes smelled like a hippie's meditation room, but it was home.

Besides, where else could you experience the joy of watching scientists chase their escaped experiments across the Martian surface while yelling, "Someone catch that mutant potato!"?

Welcome to Mars: where every day is a near-death experience wrapped in red dust and questionable engineering decisions. But hey, at least the commute was interesting—if you survived it.

***

The hover-bus lurched to a stop outside the Oxygen Distribution Center, a building that looked like someone had stacked giant tin cans and called it architecture. Sara fumbled with her access card while the airlock cycled through its daily identity crisis.

"Welcome, Sara Thompson. Current atmospheric pressure: 6.518 millibars. Far less than your dating prospects" The AI system had developed a concerning sense of humor after the last update.
Inside, red warning lights flashed across her monitor bank. The oxygen recyclers were operating at 87% efficiency—not terrible, but not great when breathing wasn't optional. The Sabatier reaction system, which converted Mars' abundant CO2 into oxygen and methane, was throwing its usual morning tantrum.

"Come on, you oversized chemistry set." Sara tapped at the controls. The system responded by making a sound like a drowning kazoo.

The real challenge wasn't just making oxygen—that was Chemistry 101 with some fancy equipment. The trick was keeping it flowing when Mars threw its weather tantrums. With atmospheric pressure less than 1% of Earth's, dust storms could knock out solar panels faster than a caffeinated toddler with a hammer.

Her console beeped. Another dust storm was approaching from Acidalia Planitia, bringing winds that could hit 70 miles per hour. Not hurricane-force by Earth standards, but when the atmosphere was thinner than a politician's promises, even moderate winds could toss rocks around like confetti.

"Attention all personnel" Sara announced over the comm. "Incoming dust storm. Please secure all equipment, experimental vegetables, and Dan's garden gnomes. Yes, especially the one with the tiny space helmet."

The recycling system's efficiency dropped another percentage point. Sara pulled up the maintenance protocols on her tablet. The problem wasn't the chemistry—the catalyst was converting CO2 just fine. It was the filters. Mars dust was fine enough to get through almost anything, like that one relative who always showed up uninvited to family gatherings.

"Time to suit up," she muttered, grabbing her tool kit. Another day of crawling through maintenance tubes, arguing with machines, and trying not to think about how the only thing between her and the vacuum of space was some arranged metal and plastic.

***

Sara squeezed through the maintenance shaft, her suit scraping against the metal walls. The oxygen recycling system's inner workings sprawled before her like a mad scientist's plumbing project. At its heart lay the catalyst chamber where CO2 underwent the Sabatier reaction—a process that would have made her high school chemistry teacher proud, if he hadn't been so busy telling her that memorizing the periodic table was more important than her "silly space dreams."

"Filter access panel B-7," she mumbled, consulting her tablet. The panel looked like it had been sandblasted by a vengeful deity. Mars dust had worked its way into every crevice, turning the original silver surface into a rust-colored mess. The particles, averaging less than 3 micrometers in diameter, were fine enough to make Earth dust look like boulders in comparison.

A crackle came over her comm. "Hey Sara, quick question." It was Dan. "If we're Martians now, do we need to file interplanetary taxes?"

"Kind of busy here, Dan." She wrestled with a stuck bolt. "Unless the IRS has figured out how to audit people 140 million miles away."

The filter assembly finally came loose, revealing the real problem. The electrostatically charged plates meant to trap dust particles had accumulated so much iron oxide that they looked like modern art installations. Mars' magnetic field, or rather its lack of one, meant the planet's surface was bombarded with radiation that turned everything into a static-charged dust magnet.

"Well, that's just great." Sara pulled out her specialized vacuum tool. The device, designed for Martian maintenance, used opposing electromagnetic fields to collect the ferromagnetic dust particles. It was a very expensive, very scientific Dustbuster.

As she worked, the storm outside intensified. The wind howled against the facility's walls, carrying particles that had last seen daylight when dinosaurs roamed Earth. The atmospheric pressure sensor dropped another fraction, reading 6.1 millibars—about the same pressure you'd find 35 kilometers above Earth's surface. It was like trying to breathe at three times the height of Mount Everest, except with better Wi-Fi.

***

Sara paused her work, the vacuum tool humming in her gloved hands. The mention of dinosaurs in her mind sparked an unexpected train of thought. She pictured a T-Rex trying to navigate the low gravity environment, its massive form bouncing across the rusty landscape in ungainly leaps.

"That would've been a sight." She snorted, the sound echoing in her helmet.

The dust continued to swirl outside as she imagined what Martian dinosaurs might have looked like. They'd need different adaptations - thicker skin to handle the radiation, specialized lungs to process the thin atmosphere. Maybe they'd have developed electromagnetic organs to deal with the solar storms, like some bizarre combination of reptile and compass.

"You still there, Sara?" Dan's voice crackled through the comm. "You went quiet."
"Just thinking about Martian dinosaurs."
"Like, actual ones or-"
"No, theoretical ones. The gravity here's about 38% of Earth's. Can you imagine what that would do to evolution? Everything could grow bigger without collapsing under its own weight."
She shifted her position in the cramped maintenance shaft, her knees protesting against the hard surface. The dust storm intensified, pelting the outer walls with ancient particles that might have seen a very different Mars - one with liquid water on the surface, before the planet lost its magnetic field and its atmosphere was stripped away by solar winds.

"They'd need to be built like pressure suits," she continued, more to herself than to Dan. "Self-contained. Maybe with crystalline shells to protect against UV radiation." The image in her head morphed from traditional dinosaurs to something more alien - creatures that looked more like living spacecraft than terrestrial reptiles.

The vacuum tool sputtered, pulling her back to reality. The filter still needed cleaning, and Martian dinosaurs weren't going to help maintain the colony's oxygen supply. Still, the thought lingered: what secrets lay buried under all this red dust? What stories could Mars tell, if they just knew where to look?

COMMUTING – WHEN PHYSICS HAS A SENSE OF HUMOR

"Finally!" Sara exclaimed, patting her hover-bike, Betsy. After two weeks of repairs that cost more than her first car on Earth, Betsy was ready to roll. The mechanic had promised it would work this time, though he'd said that with the same conviction he'd used when telling her Mars-grown coffee wouldn't taste like battery acid. (Spoiler alert: it did.)

"Okay, Betsy," She whispered to the bike, "let's not make me float away today. I'm wearing my good spacesuit, and you know how hard it is to get red dust out of the premium fabric."

The first few minutes were glorious. It was a feeling coolnes for once, zipping across the Martian landscape like a proper space explorer. That's when she hit a rock or was it a scull from an extinct alien?.

"Oh no, no, no, NO—" Sara's protests grew fainter as she separated from Betsy, achieving what could only be described as an interpretive dance routine in low gravity. Thirty feet up, she had an excellent view of the morning commute below.

Her comm crackled: "Morning: Taking the scenic route today?"
"Dan, I swear to Earth, if you're recording this—"

"Me? Never!" Dan's voice dripped with innocence. "Though you might want to check MarsBook later. Your triple backflip was *chef's kiss*."

While floating, Sara counted three other commuters in similar predicaments. They'd formed an impromptu support group, sharing snacks and comparing hover-vehicle repair bills.

Twenty minutes and one embarrassing rescue later, (the recovery team now had her on speed dial), and old Betsy had to visit the repair shop, AGAIN. She decided to cut her losses and take public transport, So she trudged to the nearest public hover-bus stop.

The station's screen displayed:
"Next bus arriving in: ¯_(ツ)_/¯ Martian minutes."

She squeezed onto the packed public transport next to a kid holding what appeared to be a solar system crafted from old air filters and something that might have started life as a potato.

"Impressive project," Sara commented.
"Thanks! It's supposed to be accurate, but Pluto keeps floating away. Just like my dad's hairpiece in the gym's low-gravity zone."

The AI-driver's voice crackled over the speakers: "Folks, we're experiencing a slight delay due to... *checks notes*... gravitational fluctuations. Or as I like to call it, Mars throwing a temper tantrum."

That's when the dust storm hit. Red particles swirled around the like angry cosmic glitter. The vehicle started performing moves that would make a break-dancer jealous.

"Ladies and gentlemen," the AI-driver announced with suspicious cheerfulness, "please ensure your gravity boots are activated. And if anyone finds a floating lunch box, it's mine. It has 'Mars' Most

Reliable Navigator' written on it."

Sara watched in fascination as the kid's solar system project rearranged itself. Mercury was now orbiting Jupiter, and Mars had somehow ended up in the kid's hoodie pocket.

By the time it reached her stop, Sara's hair resembled the aftermath of an electrical shock, and the kid's solar system model had been rearranged.—Pluto was now somehow between Earth and Venus.

Her coworker Alex, ever the show-off, arrived at work in his fancy new personal transport drone. "You should upgrade, Sara. So much more dignified than—" The drone chose that moment to hiccup, spinning like a deranged top before depositing Alex headfirst into the experimental cactus garden.

"Real dignified, Alex," Sara smirked, helping him extract various spines from his suit. "Does your drone come with complementary first aid, or is that an extra feature?"

Inside the Oxygen Distribution Center, Sara's boss greeted her with: "You're late."
"Sorry, got caught in a gravity well."
"Again? That's the third time this week."
"It's only the second. Monday was because of the escaped experimental bouncing potatoes blocking the transit tunnel."

Just another morning commute on Mars, where physics was more of a suggestion than a law, and getting to work was an extreme sport. At least she had good stories for her Earth family's weekly video calls—though they still didn't believe the one about the floating traffic jam caused by someone's escaped pet rock collection.

***

Sara slumped into her chair at the oxygen control panel, brushing off the stubborn red dust that had infiltrated her suit's "dust-proof" seals. The main display showed oxygen levels across the colony's sectors - a rainbow of numbers and graphs that determined whether everyone got to keep breathing for another day.

"System alert: CO2 scrubber three showing decreased efficiency," the computer announced in its maddeningly calm voice.

"Of course it is." Sara pulled up the diagnostics. The scrubber's efficiency had dropped to 82% - still functional, but not ideal when dealing with something as crucial as breathing. The Sabatier reaction running in the system, converting CO2 back into oxygen, needed precise conditions. Too hot or too cold, and the whole process would go sideways faster than a rover on black ice.

"Hey, Sara!" Dan's face appeared on her screen. "Quick question - is it normal for the hydroponic bay's humidity to hit 90%? Because we've got tomatoes doing synchronized swimming down here."

She checked the atmospheric controls. The recent dust storm had clogged several external vents, creating a mini tropical paradise in what was supposed to be a controlled growing environment. The irony of having too much water on Mars, where they had to mine ice caps for their H2O supply, wasn't lost on her.

"The storm messed with the condensation cycles." Sara's fingers flew over the controls. "Give me a minute to - wait, why are you in hydroponics?"

"Testing my theory that Martian-grown peppers might make decent hot sauce. So far, they're more 'mild inconvenience' than 'hot'."

The humidity issue resolved itself just as another alert popped up - pressure fluctuations in Sector 7. Sara wondered if this was what air traffic controllers on Earth felt like, except instead of planes, she juggled oxygen molecules and the occasional rogue experiment from the science department.

"At least the gravity's stabilized," she muttered, right before a coffee mug floated past her head, leaving a trail of recycled coffee in its wake.

***

Sara watched the coffee droplets dance through the low-gravity environment, making a mental note to add "floating beverage hazards" to her next safety report. The end of her shift approached, and she pulled up the colony's transit schedule on her tablet.

"Red dust storm warning for Transit Route B," flashed across her screen. Great. The hover-buses (automated transport pods) that connected the residential domes to the work sectors would be running at quarter speed. Again.

She remembered her Silicon Valley commutes - hours crawling along Highway 101, watching self-driving Teslas zip past in their special lanes while she contemplated if living in a converted storage unit was worth the astronomical rent. Back then, she'd dreamed of Mars as an escape from traffic.

"Transit Pod 7 delayed due to atmospheric interference," the system announced.

"What's the atmospheric interference code for this time?" Sara asked the computer.

"Dust accumulation on guidance sensors requires manual cleaning. Estimated delay: forty-seven minutes."

She glanced at the pod camera feed. The sleek transport vehicle sat motionless on its magnetic track, its once-white exterior stained rust-red. A maintenance bot rolled toward it, its brushes already extending to clear the sensors.

"Remember when traffic meant actual cars?" Dan's voice crackled over the intercom. "Now we're stuck waiting for robots to wash windows in space."
"At least we don't have to worry about someone cutting us off in the passing lane."

Sara checked the alternative routes. Pod 12 on Route C was running, but it meant a detour through the agricultural dome. "Though I never thought I'd miss honking horns. These pods just sit there, judging us silently."
The maintenance bot finished its work, and Pod 7 hummed back to life. Sara gathered her tablet and the now-empty coffee mug, securing both in her bag. The pod would move at a crawl through the storm, but at least she'd have a front-row seat to the swirling crimson clouds outside - a far cry from staring at brake lights on Earth.

WEATHER - MARTIAN DUST STORMS: THE WORST EXCUSE FOR A DAY OFF

Sara's alarm screeched at 6:30 AM Mars Standard Time (or as colonists called it, "Too Early O'Clock").

She fumbled for her comm panel, squinting at the flashing alert:

> **EMERGENCY WEATHER UPDATE**:
> Massive dust storm approaching!
> Essential personnel must report for duty.
> Non-essential personnel can enjoy their involuntary exfoliation.
> Have a RED-tastic day!

"Of course it's a dust storm," Sara groaned into her pillow. "Because Mars forbid we have a normal day where things just stay where we put them."

HONK! WHEEZE! SOMETHING THAT MIGHT BE MUSIC

"And there's Timmy, next door neighbors kid, with his morning tuba practice," Sara muttered. "Because what every dust storm needs is a soundtrack."

Suiting up for outside was like preparing for a spacewalk through a blender. Sara layered up: thermal underwear (because Mars couldn't decide if it wanted to be a freezer or a sauna), pressure suit (to keep her insides where they belonged), and the outer shell (a full-body dust repellent that attracted dust like a cosmic magnet).

She hesitated, then grabbed her spacesuit parka. The weather report said -60°C, but Mars was like a teenager with a mood disorder – you never knew what you'd get.
Stepping outside, Sara regretted every life choice that had led to this moment. The temperature had somehow jumped to "surface of the sun" levels.

"Really, Mars? REALLY?" She was now cooking in her own personal space sauna. "I checked the weather ten minutes ago!"

The wind picked up, sending various objects flying past:- Three lawn chairs - Someone's laundry (sorry, Johnson family) - Dan's prized collection of Earth garden gnomes (all, still, named Neil Armstrong) - Something that resembled the colony director's toupee.

At the Oxygen Distribution Center, her colleague Alex greeted her with his usual charm. "Another beautiful day in paradise, eh? I enjoy how the dust is now sentient and plotting against us."
"I signed up to be an engineer," Sara sighed, "not a professional dust-watcher."

Throughout the day, the chaos reports rolled in:

> **COLONY UPDATES**:
> ##%¤....
> Hydroponics reports all vegetables now taste like Mars (crunchy and red)
> School cancelled: All digital equipment is now analog (covered in dust)

> Dan's air filtration system has achieved consciousness and chosen violence
> The gym's anti-gravity chamber is now just... gravity
> Colony's hair gel supplies limited due to static electricity crisis

"Help!" Dan's panicked voice crackled over the comm. "My super-expensive air filter just turned into a dust cannon! It's redecorating my apartment in Early Martian Apocalypse style!"
Sara keyed her mic: "Dan, did you read the manual this time?"
"...There was a manual?"
By shift's end, Sara had witnessed:- Three tumbling rovers - One floating greenhouse - Two impromptu dust dune skiing competitions - And what appeared to be Timmy's tuba soaring through the red haze, still somehow honking

The evening brought a new colony announcement:

> **ATTENTION RESIDENTS**:
> Tomorrow is mandatory colony cleaning day!
> Bring your own shovel and a positive attitude!
> Remember: Red dust is just Mars giving you a hug!
> P.S. - If anyone finds Director Johnson's hairpiece, please return it. He claims it's "irreplaceable."

As Sara lay in bed, listening to the storm howl and Timmy somehow retrieving his tuba for more practice, her comm pinged one last time. It was Dan:
"Hey, quick question: if my air filter has gained consciousness, do I need to pay it overtime?"

Sara stared at her ceiling, Where red dust was forming what seemed to be ancient Martian curse words. Just another day on the Red Planet, where the weather forecast was always "dusty with a chance of chaos," and job descriptions included "professional dust wrangler" whether you wanted them to or not.
At least tomorrow couldn't be worse.

(Narrator: Tomorrow was, in fact, worse.)

***

Sara drifted into sleep, her mind spinning like the red dust outside. But dreams on Mars? They weren't your typical Earth variety of falling teeth or showing up naked to work. No, Martian dreams came with their own special brand of crazy.

In her dream, Sara floated through the colony's corridors - except gravity decided to work sideways. The walls became floors, and everyone walked on them like it was normal. Dan's collection of garden gnomes marched past in formation, each wearing tiny spacesuits and carrying protest signs that read "Equal Rights for Ceramic citizens!"

The low Martian gravity had warped her subconscious in ways Earth psychiatrists hadn't planned for. People didn't fall in her dreams anymore - they bounced. Sometimes right through the dome, waving as they pinwheeled into space.

"Did you file your anti-gravity paperwork?" Dream-Alex appeared, typing on a keyboard made of compressed Mars dust. "The void requires all floating to be documented in triplicate."

Her dream-self passed the hydroponics bay, where potatoes grew upside down and carrots had evolved into small orange spaceships. They launched themselves from their soil beds, leaving tiny contrails of fertilizer behind.
"The vegetables are escaping again!" Dream-Dan chased after them with a butterfly net. "They're heading for Phobos! Someone call space traffic control!"

The scene shifted to the colony's main plaza, where Director Johnson's toupee had established its own sovereign nation and was demanding diplomatic recognition from Earth. It sat atop a throne made of static-charged hair gel bottles, issuing decrees in perfect Shakespearean English.

"Wherefore art thou still using regular shampoo?" it proclaimed to a crowd of attentive dust bunnies.
Timmy's tuba floated by, playing what sounded like a jazz fusion of "Twinkle Twinkle Little Star" and Martian wind noises. The garden gnomes had formed a conga line behind it, their ceramic feet click-clacking against the metal floors.

Dreams on Mars were less about processing daily stress and more about embracing the absolute absurdity of living on a planet that seemed determined to turn everything into a red-tinted comedy show. Even in sleep, Mars refused to let its residents forget they'd chosen to live on a cosmic dust bowl with a sense of humor.

RELATIONSHIPS AND SOCIAL LIFE - DATING AND FAMILY DRAMA ON MARS

Sara checked her reflection one last time, attempting to tame her static-charged hair that made her look like she'd just stuck her finger in an electrical socket. "Perfect," she muttered. "Nothing says 'date night' like Einstein-chic."

The dust storm outside was doing her a favor for once. Kyle, her first date in months (Mars time, which felt like decades in Earth time), would be too busy not getting swept away to notice she looked like a science experiment gone wrong.

She'd met Kyle at "Martian Mingles," the colony's attempt at a singles night. The event's slogan was "Because your options are limited to people within this dome." Kyle had won her over by managing to grow strawberries that only tasted 60% like despair – a miracle by Mars standards.

The Red Planet Bistro (motto: "Earth food, Mars taste, Lower your expectations") was the colony's only restaurant. Sara spotted Kyle near the window, which offered a romantic view of what looked like the inside of a red vacuum cleaner bag.

"Sorry I'm late," Sara said, settling into her anti-gravity chair. "Had a bit of a floating incident. You know how it is – one minute you're walking, the next you're giving tours of the dome ceiling."
Kyle laughed. "Been there. Last week I sneezed during a hydroponic inspection and ended up watering the plants with my face."

The menu featured Mars's finest cuisine:
- Dehydrated Delight Salad (Now with 30% less dust!)
- Mystery Meat Surprise (The surprise is we don't know either!)
- Authentic Earth-style Pizza* (*Made with ingredients that once saw a picture of pizza)

Kyle reached for Sara's hand across the table—a nice gesture that quickly transformed into an impromptu aerial ballet as a waiter bumped into their table, launching them into a graceful ascent, hands still clasped together.
"Well," Kyle grinned, "I always hoped my first date would sweep me off my feet."
Once gravity remembered its job, things were going great until Kyle dropped The Question: "So... what's your monthly oxygen consumption like?"

Sara almost choked on her maybe-peas. On Mars, this was the equivalent of asking about someone's credit score on a first date. Real smooth, Kyle.

"Oh, you know," she deflected, "just the usual. I try to keep my breathing to a minimum."

Their conversation was interrupted by the nightly dome-announcement:

> **ATTENTION RESIDENTS**:
> Tonight's artificial sunset will be delayed due to technical difficulties.

> Please pretend it's romantic twilight for another hour.
> Also, has anyone seen Director Johnson's toupee? It was last spotted heading towards Olympus Mons.

The next morning, Sara was awakened by her neighbors' argument through the intercom:
Cara: "Jax, the replicator is making everything taste like feet again!"
Jax: "I'm fixing the solar panels! Do you want electricity or edible food?"
Cara: "Bold of you to assume anything from that replicator was ever edible!"
Sara grabbed her comm: "Guys, it's too early for relationship drama in surround sound."
Later, attempting to document her Martian life for social media, Sara spent thirty minutes trying to take a selfie where she didn't look like she'd been attacked by a red glitter bomb.
She eventually posted:
> Just living my best Mars life!
> #MartianProblems #GravityOptional #WhyIsEverythingRed
> P.S. If anyone finds my left shoe (lost during yesterday's gravity hiccup), please return. It's the only one not filled with dust.

As Sara prepared for her second date with Kyle (this time to anti-gravity yoga – nothing said romance like kicking your date in the face), she reflected on Martian relationships. Sure, they had unique challenges:
- Oxygen bill discussions on first dates
- Spontaneous floating incidents
- Hair that defied physics
- The constant threat of death by decompression
- Food that tasted like regret
- Dan next door still trying to grow hair using cosmic radiation

But hey, at least there was no awkward "What do you do?" small talk. Everyone was just trying not to die on a different planet.

Besides, Kyle had promised to show her his secret stash of actual Earth coffee beans. On Mars, that was a marriage proposal.

***

Sara stared at her reflection in the polished metal surface of her bathroom mirror. The Martian gravity, about 38% of Earth's, made her hair float in weird directions despite her best attempts to tame it. At least the lower gravity meant her joints didn't ache as much after a long day of maintaining the colony's oxygen systems.

The date with Kyle would have to wait. Her comm unit buzzed with an urgent message about pressure differentials in Dome Section C. The technical challenge of maintaining livable conditions on Mars never took a day off. The atmospheric pressure on Mars averaged around 6 millibars - compared to Earth's 1,013 millibars at sea level - which meant even a tiny breach could spell disaster.

"Of course this happens now." Sara grabbed her toolkit and headed for the maintenance corridor. The rusty Martian dust had worked its way into another seal, a common problem that kept engineers like her employed. The fine particles, averaging about 3 micrometers in diameter, were small enough to infiltrate any system.

Dan poked his head around the corner as she passed. "Hey neighbor! Want to join our Martian meteorite collection club? We found one that looks like Elvis!"
"Kind of busy preventing explosive decompression right now." Sara ducked under a low-hanging pipe. "Maybe next time?"

The maintenance corridor smelled like ozone and recycled air. The colony's air filtration system processed everything from human breath to plant transpiration, turning it back into breathable oxygen through a complex series of chemical reactions. Sara often joked that she could taste Tuesday's lunch coming back through the vents on Thursday.

She reached the problematic seal, where the red dust had indeed created a microscopic gap. As she worked, the colony's daily announcement system crackled to life:

Attention residents: Today's UV index is:
Why Are You Even Outside?
Please remember that Mars receives about 43% of the sunlight Earth does, but with almost no ozone layer, you'll still cook faster than those mysterious protein packs in the cafeteria.
Also, has anyone seen Director Johnson's other shoe? It was last spotted near the hydroponic bay trying to escape the artificial gravity field.

HEALTH AND FITNESS - WORKING OUT IN MARTIAN GRAVITY

Sara stared at the "Red Planet Fitness Center" sign, which now read: "WHERE EVERY DAY IS … G….. DAY" (because some letters had floated away during the last dust storm). Below it, someone had scrawled: "Gravity Optional, Laughter Mandatory."

Inside, the gym resembled the aftermath of a collision between a circus and a physics experiment. In one corner, Brad from Accounting was bench-pressing what appeared to be a paper clip, grunting like he was lifting a truck. On the treadmills, people weren't so much running as performing an interpretive dance titled "Kangaroo Having an Identity Crisis."

"Morning, Sara!" Dan called, attempting sit-ups while tied down with enough straps to secure a spacecraft. "Ready for another day of pretending we're not morphing into human marshmallows?"

The gym offered various specialized programs:
- Anti-Gravity Abs (Now with 90% less gravity!)
- Floating HIIT (High-Intensity Intermittent Tumbling)
- Martian Marathon Training (Catch your breath before it floats away!)
- Extreme Sitting (Harder than it sounds)

Sara grabbed a dumbbell that would've been heavy on Earth. Here, it felt like lifting a ambitious balloon. "Remember when working out was about getting stronger?" she panted, curling the weight. "Now it's about not launching yourself through the ceiling."

"Tell me about it," Dan replied, still bouncing through sit-ups. "I video-called my grandma yesterday. She challenged me to an arm-wrestling match—and she would have won. She's 92 and uses bridge as her workout routine."

Next up: "Low-G Yoga" with Instructor Moonbeam (real name: Barbara from Wisconsin, but nobody was zen enough for that). The class description read: "Find your center... wherever it floats to."

Moonbeam drifted into class in a cloud of essential oils (which, in low gravity, created an actual cloud that followed her around). "Welcome, Earth souls trapped in Martian bodies," she intoned. "Today we'll explore the intersection between inner peace and outer space."
What followed was less yoga and more like a game of human pinball:
- Downward Dog became Upward Yeet
- Warrior Pose turned into Wandering Pose
- Child's Pose resulted in three collision reports
- Tree Pose? More like Free-falling Pose

"Remember," Moonbeam called as chaos unfolded, "embrace the float. Become one with the void. And please fill out the liability waiver before attempting headstands."

Sara's "relaxing" session resulted in:
- 3 accidental headbutts
- 1 tangled yoga mat incident
- 2 cases of mistaken identity while floating upside down
- 1 small cut from an enthusiastic high-five with Dan that turned

into a low-orbit high-five

The next day at the medical center, Dr. Martinez ("Keeping colonists alive despite their best efforts") examined Sara's swollen hand.
"Let me guess," she said, "another yoga casualty?"
"Warrior Pose turned into Warrior Emergency."

The doctor applied some high-tech bandages. "Good news: you'll live. Bad news: you're developing what we call 'Martian Muscle Memory' – your body's now better at floating than walking."

New injuries required new treatments:
- Anti-gravity bandages (to keep the bandage on the wound, not floating beside it)
- Red dust-resistant antiseptic (because everything on Mars needed dust protection)
- Extra rehabilitation exercises (like "controlled floating" and "intentional falling")

The colony's medical records now included unique categories:
- Yoga-Related Incidents
- Treadmill Trajectories Gone Wrong
- Unexpected Ceiling Encounters
- High-Five Injuries (Low Gravity Division)

On her way home, Sara passed the new sports complex where colonists were inventing Martian versions of Earth sports:
- Low-G Basketball (More like "Try to catch the floating ball while also floating")
- Martian Soccer (90 minutes of people drifting after a ball)
- Anti-Gravity Tennis (people just spinning in circles)
- Extreme Standing Still (An Olympic-level event on Mars)

"Hey, Sara!" someone called out. "We're inventing Martian 'Skyball'—or 'Marsian Broom League,' as someone decided to name

it!
Want to join? No brooms required—you float naturally!"

Looking at the chaos of people bouncing around like zero-gravity pinballs, Sara grinned. "Why not? It's not like I have to worry about breaking a sweat!"
As she launched herself into the game, Sara reflected on Martian fitness:
- Every movement was an adventure
- Gravity was more of a suggestion than a law
- Exercise equipment needed seat belts
-"Getting ripped" meant something entirely different when you could lift a rover with one hand
- But at least no one could tell if you skipped leg day

Wasn't that what staying healthy on Mars was all about? Finding joy in the absurdity, strength in the struggle, and humor in the daily battle against becoming a floating marshmallow?

Plus, she was pretty sure she was developing superhuman powers. Sure, they only worked in 0.37g, but still – progress!

***

Sara's newfound "super-strength" came with a catch
- Earth's gravity would crush her like a soda can if she returned. The colony's medical team had calculated that for every year on Mars, colonists lost about 3% of their bone density despite their rigorous exercise routines. Sara pulled up the latest bone scan on her tablet, wincing at the numbers.

"Your skeleton's going tourist mode," Dan commented, peering over her shoulder. "All that calcium just taking a vacation."
"Thanks for that scientific analysis, Dr. Dan."
Sara scrolled through her medical report. The data showed her muscles adapting to Mars' 0.37g environment

- getting longer, more efficient at low-resistance movements, but weaker by Earth standards.

The colony's gym added new warning signs weekly:
CAUTION: Your perceived strength is not your Earth strength
WARNING: Jumping jacks may result in ceiling contact
REMINDER: What goes up... keeps going up

Their latest exercise innovation involved resistance suits that simulated Earth-like conditions. Sara stepped into hers, feeling like she'd been wrapped in concrete. The suit compressed her joints and muscles, fighting against every movement.

"These things feel like trying to swim through peanut butter," she wheezed, attempting basic arm circles. The suit's internal sensors monitored her movements, adjusting pressure to maintain Earth-like resistance.

The colony's medical staff had developed a detailed chart of "**Martian Body Changes**" which hung in every exercise room:
- Spine elongation (Everyone gained about 2 inches in height)
- Fluid redistribution (Leading to what colonists called "Mars Face" - puffy features)
- Decreased blood volume (Making everyone look like they'd skipped leg decade, not just leg day)
- Enhanced floating ability (Not actually a medical term, but everyone insisted on including it)

"At least we're all getting taller," Dan said, stretching his elongated spine. "Though I'm pretty sure my mom won't recognize me in video calls anymore - my head's is a perfect circle now."

Sara checked her heart rate monitor. On Mars, her heart had adapted to pumping blood with less effort, making Earth's gravity seem like trying to push molasses uphill through a coffee stirrer.

MARTIAN ECONOMY – JOBS, BILLS, AND THE COST OF LIVING

Sara glared at her monthly financial statement, which read like a dystopian shopping list:

> **MONTHLY CHARGES**: >

> Basic Oxygen Package: 500 Credits
> Premium Air Quality Surcharge: 200 Credits
> Emergency Oxygen Insurance: 150 Credits
> "Just In Case You Need To Breathe" Fee: 75 Credits
> Red Dust Removal Service: 300 Credits
> Gravity Compensator Rental: 250 Credits
> Existence on Mars Tax: 1,000 Credits
> "Because We Can" Administrative Fee: 125 Credits
> **TOTAL**: Way Too Much

"I left Earth to escape bills," Sara muttered, "not to find new ways to pay for everything, including the right to exist in space."

As Martian Oxygen Distribution Manager (or "Professional Air Traffic Controller for Molecules"), Sara's job involved:
- Telling people they couldn't have more oxygen
- Explaining why they couldn't have more oxygen
- Running from people angry about not getting more oxygen
- Hiding from Dave from Dome 3 who kept trying to

barter his crypto for extra air

Her comm panel buzzed with the daily announcements:

> **ATTENTION MARTIANS**: >
> 1. Tomorrow is a minimal-oxygen day
> (Yes, we know you need to breathe. No, complaining won't help)
> 2. Solar panel cleaning fees are increasing
> (Dust doesn't clean itself, people)
> 3. Dave, stop mining MarsCoin
> (You're using more electricity than the entire northern hemisphere)
> 4. New investment opportunity: MarsArtisanal Air
> (It's just regular air in a fancy container)

Speaking of Dave, his latest venture was "MarsCoin" – because what a planet with limited oxygen needed was another way to waste electricity. His marketing pitch: "It's like Bitcoin, but redder!"

Sara's investment portfolio was a journey through bad decisions:
- Algae Farms Inc. (As of now, worth less than actual algae)
- Red Dust Collections Ltd. (Turns out, Mars has plenty already)
- Oxygen Futures (Because gambling on air seemed smart at the time)
- Dave's MarsCoin (She bought at the peak, just before the Solar Flare Crash)

Her comm pinged with messages:
Dan: "Can I trade oxygen credits for premium Martian soil? It's extra red today!"
Sara: "Dan, you can't trade oxygen. Remember last time?"
Dan: "The party was worth the temporary unconsciousness!"

The Mars Central Bank's latest offerings included:
- The "Breathe Easy" Loan Program
- The "Pay-Per-Gasp" Payment Plan

- The "Air Now, Pay Later" Credit Scheme
- The "Oxygen Rewards" Credit Card
(Earn 2% back on all breathing-related purchases!)

Job opportunities on Mars were... unique. Sara scrolled through the listings:

> **HELP WANTED**:
> Professional Dust Herder ("Must be able to convince dust to move in specific directions")
> Vegetable Therapist ("Our tomatoes have trust issues")
> Gravity Compliance Officer ("Keep things down when they should be down")
> MarsCoin Recovery Specialist ("Help Dave find his lost digital wallet")
> Professional Oxygen Conservationist ("Teaching colonists to talk less and breathe less")

The Martian Stock Exchange wasn't helping:
- Algae Futures: ↓ 90%
- Dust Mining Corp: ↑ 200% (Thanks, storm season!)
- Oxygen Industries: Too volatile to measure
- Dave's Latest Venture: File not found

New business ventures popped up daily:
- "Red Planet Retreats" (Renting out premium dust-viewing spots)
- "Air Bottles & Bubbles" (selling air in fancy bottles)
- "Martini Martian Bar" (Serving algae-based cocktails that tasted like regret)
- "Zero-G Zone" (Low-G entertainment center— closed due to too many floating incidents)

Sara's budgeting app categorized her expenses:
- Essential: Oxygen, Water, Gravity
- Semi-Essential: Food, Shelter, Communications
- Luxury: Earth Imports, Extra Breathing, Hopes, Dreams - Why

Did You Buy This: MarsCoin Investment

As she prepared for bed, another announcement blared:

> **BREAKING NEWS**:
> Due to recent economic fluctuations, we're introducing a new currency: O_2Coins
> Exchange rate: 1 breath = 1 O_2Coin
> Note: Hyperventilating to earn more coins is prohibited

Sara chuckled, setting her alarm for another day of oxygen management and financial gymnastics. At least on Mars, when your bank account hit zero, you could blame it on the gravity.

Plus, she'd just received her monthly salary:- 50% in MarsCoin (worth less than Monopoly money) - 30% in Oxygen Credits (non-transferable, non-refundable, non-sensical) - 20% in Real Money (immediately spent on breathing)

Welcome to the Martian economy: Where the air is precious, the dust is free, and somehow, Dave is still trying to make cryptocurrency happen.

***

The next morning, Sara faced her daily challenge: explaining basic thermodynamics to colonists who thought they could just "make more air." The Martian atmosphere, at less than 1% of Earth's pressure, meant every molecule counted.

"No, we can't just 'open a window' when it gets stuffy," she explained to a new arrival. "Unless you want your eyeballs to boil at 0.087 psi."
The colony's air recycling system hummed behind her, converting carbon dioxide back to oxygen through a complex process that somehow still couldn't keep up with Dave's crypto mining rigs.

The system used state-of-the-art molecular sieves, which Sara had modified after discovering that Martian dust particles were small enough to slip through standard Earth filters – a fact she learned when the entire Dome 2 turned orange last spring.

"And here's why we can't just plant more trees," Sara pointed to her presentation slides. "The soil's perchlorates would poison Earth plants faster than my last relationship." The toxic salts in Martian soil meant everything had to be grown in treated containers, leading to the great Tomato Shortage of '43 when someone used the wrong fertilizer.

Her comm beeped with another crisis:
"The gravity sensors are acting up again," Dan messaged. "The coffee machine thinks it's on Jupiter. It's making everything extra strong."

The reduced Martian gravity, about 38% of Earth's, played havoc with equipment calibrated for Earth. Last week, the automatic doors had started opening with enough force to launch people across corridors, leading to what the colony now referred to as "The Great Hallway Olympics."

"At least the lower gravity means we use less energy moving around," Sara muttered, checking the oxygen consumption rates. "Though it doesn't help when people keep trying to start low-g dance parties."

The reality of Mars colonization meant dealing with radiation levels that made microchips glitch, pervasive dust that contained enough static electricity to power a small fan, and temperatures that swung from a balmy -63°C to a toasty 20°C during summer days. Sara's engineering degree hadn't prepared her for explaining why they couldn't just "sweep the dust outside" without creating an electromagnetic storm that would fry their communications.

FOOD – THE MARTIAN DIET: HOW TO GROW (OR REGROW) YOUR DINNER

Sara's kitchen looked like a mad scientist's lab, if that scientist was into cooking and desperate. Her fridge contained various shades of "probably food" ranging from suspicious red to concerning purple. But the real showstopper was her greenhouse, taking up so much space she had to put her bed in the kitchen. "Home is where the herbs are," as the Mars Colony brochure cheerfully lied.

"Okay, let's see what mutant vegetables we're dealing with today," Sara mumbled, approaching her crops with the caution of someone who'd once been attacked by an overachieving zucchini plant.

First stop: the potato section. Sara had spent weeks getting the molecular settings just right, triple-checking everything. "Please be normal, please be normal," she chanted, pulling back the leaves.

"Oh, come ON!"

Where reasonable potatoes should have been, she found what looked like spud bodybuilders. Each potato was the size of a small car tire. "Wonderful. Just wonderful." I finally get the shape right, and now they're on steroids."

Moving to her herb garden, Sara leaned in to sniff the basil. Bad move. "Holy—! Why do you smell like Dan's gym locker?" She glared at the plants. "You had ONE job!"

Her comm panel pinged:

> **COLONY ANNOUNCEMENT**:
> From the Cafeteria Today's Daily Special
> Mars Mystery Meat Monday
> Now with 60% less mystery, 40% more... meat-adjacent proteins
> Served with our famous color-changing lettuce!
> *Management not responsible for any sudden urges to yodel*

Just then, Dan burst through her door, wearing his "Kiss the Mad Scientist" apron. "Sara! You won't believe what I've done with the mealworms!"
"Dan, the last time you said that, we had to evacuate the entire floor."
"No, no, this is different! I've created..." he paused, "SPACE BACON!"
Sara eyed the wiggling container in his hands. "That's still moving, Dan."
"That's how you know it's fresh!"

Sara looked at her mutant potatoes, then at her foot-scented herbs, and then at Dan's enthusiastic face. "Fine. But if I start glowing in the dark again..."
"That only happened once, and the doctor said it would fade away!"

They set up their "test kitchen" (aka Sara's counter space). Dan's creation looked like bacon if it had an identity crisis and decided to become a disco ball. It sparkled. Food shouldn't sparkle.
"I call it 'Breakfast at Phobos,'" Dan announced.
Just then, Sara's prized Earth coffee beans (which cost her a month's oxygen rations and her firstborn child) started floating.

The artificial gravity was acting up again.
"Quick, grab them!" Sara lunged for the beans while Dan tried to catch his escaping space food. They collided mid-air, creating what could only be described as a zero-gravity food fight.

That's when Sara's boss decided to make a surprise video call.
"Thompson! Why aren't you at the—" he stopped, taking in the scene: Sara and Dan floating among sparkly bacon bits and coffee beans, with giant potatoes rolling across the floor and herbs that smelled like a locker room.
"Would you believe this is a new preservation technique?" Sara tried.
The boss sighed. "Just... try not to blow up the kitchen again. Remember the Great Pasta Incident of '47?"
The maintenance crew had needed therapy after that one.

As they cleaned up, Dan's space food stuck to the ceiling ("It'll come down."), and Sara salvaged her precious coffee beans, she couldn't help but laugh. Sure, Earth had regular-sized vegetables and non-sentient bacon, but did they have antigravity food fights?
"Hey Sara," Dan called, "want to help me with my next project? I'm working on self-dancing spaghetti!"
"Dan, no."
"Dan, yes!"

Just another day in the Martian culinary adventure, where the food was weird, the herbs had attitude problems, and somehow, they were still better than Mystery Meat Monday.

***

The next morning, Sara faced her greatest challenge yet: explaining to the Colony Board why there were sparkly, still-wiggling bacon strips decorating her ceiling like a disco-themed nightmare. The real problem wasn't the aesthetics - it was the fact that the strips had started multiplying.

"According to my calculations," Sara pointed at her tablet while floating three feet off the ground (the gravity controls were still acting up), "the mealworms Dan used somehow adapted to the lower atmospheric pressure. Mars's atmosphere is about 1% as dense as Earth's, which turns regular mealworms into party-loving replicators."
The biochemistry lab reported that the worms had developed a unique survival mechanism. In the thin Martian atmosphere, consisting of carbon dioxide at about 6.9 millibars of pressure, the proteins had restructured themselves to capture available moisture - making them immortal disco dancers.

"Look on the bright side," Dan chimed in through the video feed, "we've solved our protein shortage!"
The board members watched as another strip of glittering bacon detached itself and started doing what looked like the macarena.

"Thompson," Director Chen massaged his temples, "when we asked for sustainable food solutions, we didn't mean self-replicating ceiling decorations."

Sara ducked as a enthusiastic bacon strip swung past her head. "The good news is they're edible and contain 40% more protein than Earth bacon. The bad news is they refuse to be caught unless you play disco music."

The situation got more complicated when they discovered the bacon had formed a symbiotic relationship with her mutant potatoes. The spuds had started rolling themselves across the floor in rhythm with the bacon's dance moves. Mars's 0.375 G gravity meant the potato-bacon conga line could build up some serious momentum.
"We're calling it the Disco-system," Dan announced. "It's like an ecosystem, but with more Bee Gees."

Sara watched as her controlled experimental garden transformed into what could only be described as a supernatural food party. Between the anti-gravity incidents, the self-aware produce, and the fact that Mars's perchlorates in the soil had somehow given her basil a PhD in interpretive dance, she wondered if this was what mission control meant by "expect the unexpected."

ENTERTAINMENT - WHAT TO DO ON MARS WHEN YOU'RE BORED

Sara sprawled on her couch, contemplating the eternal question: "What's a Martian gal to do on a Saturday night?" The entertainment options on Mars were about as varied as the planet's color scheme – which is to say, RED.

Her entertainment console displayed the evening's options:

TONIGHT'S HIGHLIGHTS:

> Low-G Soccer Finals (Now with 60% ball retention!)
> As The Dust Storms (Season 47, Episode 394)
> Earth News (Only 3 months delayed!)
> Watch Paint Dry in 0.37 Gravity
> Dave's MarsCoin Investment Seminar
Sara's comm pinged with messages:
Alex: "Soccer finals tonight! They installed a ball retrieval system after last time's... incident."
Sara: "You mean when the ball achieved escape velocity?"
Alex: "Hey, it's passing Jupiter by now. That's kind of cool!"

MARS SPORTS NETWORK presented:

- Ping Pong Championships (Current match duration: 4 days, 7 hours)
- Floating Basketball (Renamed "Ball Chase In Space")
- Red Planet Rugby ("Like regular rugby but with more floating")
- Extreme Standing Still Competition (Current champion: Linda from Accounting)

The movie selection wasn't much better:

NOW SHOWING:

> Super heros: Final Battle Part 23: The Retirement Home
> Slow and floating 47: Mars Drift
> The Real Marswives of Olympus Mons
> Finding Alien 12: Lost In the galaxy
> (All titles subject to 3-year Earth delay, The above titles are parodies and not affiliated with any existing franchises.)

The local entertainment wasn't helping:
"As The Dust Storms"- Today's Episode:
Derek: "I used our water rations to wash my rover!
"Jessica: "But I needed that water for our algae farm!
"Derek: "The dust was ruining my Instagram aesthetics!"
Dramatic music plays while both float away in different directions

Sara flipped through

Martian TV channels:
- Martian Baking Challenge: Where the Secret Ingredient is Always Dust
- Mars' Got Weird (Featuring zero-G juggling and Martian throat-singing)
- Kolonist Chronicles (Reality dome drama: tears, tantrums, and no oxygen to cry into)
- Mars Hacks: How It's made on Mars: (Spoiler: It's all duct tape and

recycled filters)

The art scene was... unique.

The Red Planet Gallery's latest exhibition:-
- "Dust in the Wind" (just dust)
- "Gravity's Betrayal" (A floating chair)
- "Earth Memories" (A water bottle filled with tears)
- "Dave's Failed MarsCoin Mining Rig As Art"

Dan's message popped up: "Concert tonight! The Red Orbiters are playing!"?

Popular Martian bands included:
- The Red Orbiters (Hit single: "Baby, You Make My Heart Float")
- Rustronica (Heavy metal with oxygen tank percussion)
- Low-G Mars Diva (Defying gravity, one note at a time)
- Volcanic Vibrations (Not to be confused with Earth's top charts)

Top Martian Songs of the Week:
1. "Oxygen's Overrated (I Only Need Your Love)"
2. "Red Dust In My Helmet (Can't See My Baby Tonight)"
3. "999 Problems But Gravity Ain't One"
4. "Dust Storm of Love"
5. "Dave's MarsCoin Blues"

Virtual Reality experiences offered escape:
- "Earth Weather Simulator" (Experience rain without rust!)
- "Traffic Jam Simulator" (For those missing Earth commutes)
- "Regular Gravity Experience" (Warning: May cause existential crisis)
- "Dave's MarsCoin Adventure" (Sponsored content)

Popular Martian Games:
- Red D. Repressurization (Can you survive the dome leak?)
- Rover Heist: Mars Edition (Customize your rover and evade orbital law enforcement!)
- Dome Life: Survival Sim: (Build your dream dome. Or watch it

implode.)
- Grumpy Martians: Zero Gravity Chaos (Sling your Martians through wild and wacky Martian physics!)
- MartianCoin Tycoon (Built by Dave, obviously): (Dominate the interplanetary crypto market!)

Colony Event Calendar:
- Monday: Low-G Yoga
- Tuesday: Dust Art Workshop
- Wednesday: "Why Did We Come Here?" Support Group
- Thursday: Anti-Gravity Dance Class
- Friday: Emergency Drill (But Fun!)
- Saturday: Movie Night (3 Years Behind)
- Sunday: Contemplate Existence In Space

Sara decided on the new VR experience: "Mars builder 3000" (Create and shape your world with endless possibilities!). As she set up her gear, another announcement blared:

ENTERTAINMENT UPDATE:

> Due to popular demand, we're adding new VR experiences:
> "Stand In Earth Rain"
> "Pet A Dog That Isn't In A Spacesuit"
> "Experience Traffic Jams Again!"
> "Watch Dave Lose More Money On MarsCoin"

Because sometimes the best entertainment on Mars was pretending you weren't on Mars at all. Though Sara had to admit, watching Dave's crypto adventures was pretty entertaining too.

***

Sara slipped the VR headset on, but a warning flashed across her vision: "System calibration error - local gravity compensation required." She yanked it off with a groan. The colony's recent gravity fluctuations were playing havoc with everything from the entertainment systems to the coffee machines - though calling the brown sludge they produced "coffee" was being generous.

"Great. Another thing broken by Mars' 0.37g." She tapped her tablet, pulling up the day's maintenance schedule. The reduced gravity meant everything from their digestive systems to their exercise routines needed constant adjustment. Even their bones were slowly losing density, despite the mandatory two hours of resistance training each day.

The colony's latest solution to the bone density problem sat in the corner of her room - a vibration plate that simulated Earth's gravitational load. Sara called it "the torture board." It worked by sending precise frequencies through the body, stimulating osteoblast production. All she knew was it made her teeth chatter and her nose itch.

"Hey Sara!" Dan's voice crackled through her room's comm. "The hydroponics lab just reported their tomatoes are floating again. Want to help catch vegetable escapees?"
"Let me guess - another pressure differential in Greenhouse Three?"
"Bingo! Though this time it's kind of beautiful. The cherry tomatoes are orbiting the lettuce beds like tiny red moons."

Sara grabbed her tablet and headed for the greenhouse. The sight that greeted her was pure chaos - dozens of ripe tomatoes spinning through the air while frustrated botanists tried to net them with butterfly catchers. One researcher was using two heads of lettuce as makeshift ping-pong paddles.

"At least it's not as bad as the Great Potato Incident of '47," Dan said, ducking under a wayward tomato. "Remember when those spuds broke through the containment netting and we found them sprouting in the air filtration system three months later?"

Sara did remember. They'd had to update the colony's official manual with a new chapter titled "Root Vegetable Zero-G Containment Protocols." It sat right between "Emergency Decompression Procedures" and "Why Your Coffee Maker Keeps Floating Away: A Troubleshooting Guide."

***

Dan and Sara worked methodically to capture the floating tomatoes, but their butterfly nets kept tangling in the artificial breeze from the ventilation system. The red spheres danced just out of reach, taunting them with each failed swipe.

"You know what this reminds me of?" Dan asked as he swung his net at a cluster of cherry tomatoes. "That old game—Martian Tomato Chopper." Or was that just something he had dreamed up?

"Except we're trying not to slice them." Sara ducked as a large beefsteak tomato sailed over her head. "Though at this rate, we might end up with sauce anyway."

The hydroponics team had gathered quite an audience. Off-duty colonists pressed their faces against the greenhouse windows, recording the spectacle on their tablets. Someone had even started playing circus music through the colony's speaker system.

Then it happened. Dr. Wong, the colony's most serious-minded physicist, walked in carrying his lunch - a pristine peanut butter and jelly sandwich. He stopped dead in his tracks, mouth agape at the floating produce.

A rogue tomato struck his sandwich with pinpoint accuracy. The impact sent glob of grape jelly arcing through the reduced gravity, landing square on his nose. The stoic scientist crossed his eyes to stare at the purple blob.

"I suppose," he said with unexpected deadpan delivery, "this is what they mean by a Martian food fight. Though I must say, the atmospheric pressure seems a bit sauce-picious."

The entire greenhouse erupted in laughter. Even the plants seemed to shake with mirth - though that was just another gravity fluctuation. Dr. Wong's unexpected pun, combined with his perfect comic timing and jelly-decorated nose, created what would later be known in colony records as "The Great Tomato Pun-demonium of '48."
Sara wiped tears from her eyes as Dan collapsed against a hydroponic tower, wheezing with laughter. A cherry tomato bounced off his forehead, adding a perfect comedic punctuation mark to the moment.

"Well," Dr. Wong said, wiping jelly from his nose with his sleeve, "I believe this makes me a seasoned scientist."

ACTIVITIES – MARTIAN OUTDOOR ADVENTURES: FISHING AND CAMPING ON THE RED PLANET

Sara stared at her "Essential Mars Camping Checklist": On Earth, there would be even more useless stuff to pack—things that had no value on here anyway. Yet, the items essential for Mars would be pointless back on Earth.

Ha ha, the irony of trying to play the role of a survival expert.

BASIC SURVIVAL GEAR:

> Anti-radiation tent (Now with 50% less cancer!)
> Gravity-compensating sleeping bag (Stop floating while you sleep!)
> Emergency oxygen (Because breathing is nice)
> Methane-proof fishing gear (For catching... something)
> Will to live (Recommended)
> Last will and testament (Just in case)

Her comm buzzed with pre-trip messages:

Alex: "Don't forget your Martian Angler 3000!"
Sara: "You mean the expensive stick we dangle in poison lakes?"
Alex: "Hey, last time something bit the line!"
Sara: "That was Dan falling in."
Dan: "I'm bringing marshmallows!"
Sara: "we can't have fire in no oxygen."
Dan: "But I got the exclusive space ones! They only explode a little!"

The gang loaded their pressurized rover (nicknamed "Please Don't Break Down Here") with enough gear to survive several apocalypses:

CAMPING SUPPLIES:

- Regular supplies (Earth essentials)
- Mars supplies (Keeping you alive stuff)
- Dan's marshmallows (Possibly dangerous)
- Alex's Plasma-Roaster 5000 (Absolutely hazardous)
- Emergency beacon (For when everything else goes wrong)

The drive to the methane lake featured 3 near-death experiences with 2 dust devil encounters and 1 rover wheel alignment issue. Also countless "Are we there yet?" from Dan and several existential crises.

Setting up camp was like performing circus acts in space. The tent achieved flight three times and the sleeping bags tried to escape to Phobos. Dan got tangled in guy lines and almost achieved orbit and Alex's Plasma-Roaster created a small fusion reaction (could this be the start of a new business adventure, free power from marshmallows?).

Sara contemplated walking back to Earth.

MARTIAN FISHING HIGHLIGHTS:
Hour 1: Nothing

Hour 2: Still nothing
Hour 3: Dan fell in (again)
Hour 4: Something fell for their lures!

After countless minutes of battling the "beast" they landed the creature.
The catch looked like:
- 40% jellyfish
- 30% lobster
- 20% nightmare fuel
- 10% pure confusion
- 100% reason to never go fishing again
Their debate about eating it went like this:
Dan: "I bet it tastes like chicken!"
Sara: "Everything weird tastes like chicken."
Alex: "That's not even technically an animal."
Mystery Creature: *Glares judgmentally with maybe-eyes*

This was an catch and release case…….

Evening Entertainment:

- Marshmallow Russian Roulette with the Plasma-Roaster.
- "Guess That Sound" (Spoiler: It's always the rover creaking).
- "What's That Smell?" (Answer: Dan's marshmallows).
- Existential discussions about life on Mars.
- Trying to clean marshmallow goo off the helmets.

The night went on, stars sparkling in the sky and the mood was getting better and suddenly came "The Sound"
Sara: "What was that?"
Alex: "Sounded like the wind."
Dan: "There are not enough atmosphere for wind that loud!"
Everyone: *Silent panic*

The mysterious creature seemed to have:

- Size: Somewhere between "too big" and "oh no"
- Speed: Faster than their rover
- Attitude: Hungry
- Interest in humans: Uncomfortably high

New Activities Added to Trip:
- Cryptid hunting
- Speed packing
- Olympic-level running
- Prayer (regardless of religious beliefs)
- Breaking rover speed records

Sara's Post-Trip Report:

> Things I Learned:
> 1. Mars has wildlife. It's terrifying.
> 2. Marshmallows are deadly weapons in space.
> 3. Dan will try to eat anything.
> 4. Alex's inventions should be illegal.
> 5. Camping on Mars is just expensive dying.

The safety protocol stated that this should be sent to the security office for briefing.

And soon:

Colony Notice Board Update:

ATTENTION: New Tent camp area discovered! Features include:
- Scenic methane lakes - Unknown predatory wildlife
- Excellent cell service (for your last calls home)
- Premium burial plots - Visit at your own risk!"

As they sped back to the colony, something howling in the distance, Sara realized that Mars camping was less "roughing it" and more "trying not to die in creative new ways." But hey, at least they had a story for the colony newsletter:

"Local Idiots Survive Camping Trip. Discover New Apex Predator. Ruin Marshmallows Forever"

Just another weekend on Mars, where outdoor activities came

with a side of possible extinction.

***

Sara stared at the colony's incident report form on her desk, trying to figure out how to categorize "possible encounter with Martian mega-fauna" without triggering another base-wide panic. The last time that happened, they'd spent three weeks in lockdown because someone thought they saw a space unicorn. It turned out to be Dan in a silver thermal suit with an antenna stuck to his helmet.

"Under 'Species Classification,' should I put 'Big and Scary' or 'Unknown Life Form That Likes Marshmallows'?" She scratched her head, leaving red dust trails in her hair. The Martian dust had a knack for infiltrating everything - it was mostly silicon dioxide and iron oxide, which explained why her hair now looked like a rusty copper wire.

The atmospheric pressure readings from their campsite kept fluctuating in ways that defied their current understanding of Martian meteorology. At 6.1 millibars - less than one percent of Earth's pressure at sea level - Mars shouldn't have been able to support anything bigger than a microbe. Yet their sensors had picked up movement patterns suggesting something macro.

"The methane lakes could, in theory, support anaerobic life," Alex had suggested during their debrief. "The liquid methane maintains a temperature of about -161°C. Maybe whatever we saw has an antifreeze-like compound in its cells, similar to Arctic fish on Earth."

Dan had contributed by suggesting they name it "Marshmallow Muncher," since it appeared right after his explosive cooking experiment. The creature's timing had been impeccable - showing up when the Plasma-Roaster had reached its peak energy output of 2000 watts, enough power to light up their location like a cosmic birthday cake.

Sara added a note to the report: "Possible correlation between high-energy cooking appliances and apex predator attraction. Recommend ban on all future marshmallow-related activities within colony limits."

She glanced at the sample jar on her desk containing what looked like a cross between fish scales and metallic sequins - the only physical evidence they'd managed to collect from their encounter. Under the microscope, the scales showed properties unlike anything in their database. They were reflective and heat-absorbing, most likely an adaptation to Mars's extreme temperature swings of over 100°C between day and night.

***

Sara turned the scale over in her hands, watching it catch the artificial light of her office. The iridescent shimmer reminded her of the documentaries she used to watch about Earth's prehistoric creatures. Back then, she'd laughed at the idea of dinosaurs on Mars. Now? Not so much.

"You're still obsessing over that thing?" Dan poked his head through her door, his hair sticking up in all directions like he'd been experimenting with the static electricity generator again.

"I'm not obsessing. I'm conducting a thorough scientific investigation." Sara set the scale down and pulled up the thermal imaging data from that night. "Look at this heat signature. Whatever it was, it maintained a constant body temperature despite the external environment dropping to minus seventy."
"Maybe it's wearing a really good jacket." Dan plopped into the chair across from her desk, knocking over her prized collection of Mars rocks.
"Yes, Dan. It shops at "Martian Clothes: Sub-Zero Edition""

The thermal readings flickered across her screen - a massive shape, the size of a small car, moving with surprising grace for something that shouldn't exist. The data showed it circling their campsite three times before vanishing into a nearby canyon.

"You know what this means?" Sara zoomed in on the creature's distinctive thermal pattern. "We could be looking at actual Martian megafauna. Living, breathing proof that complex life evolved on Mars."

"Or..." Dan leaned forward, his expression serious for once. "We've discovered space dinosaurs."

Sara opened her mouth to argue, then stopped. The thought of Martian T-rexes stomping around the red planet's surface made her inner eight-year-old squeal with joy. She pictured them with specialized scales to regulate temperature, adapted lungs to process the thin atmosphere, maybe even-

Her train of thought derailed as she noticed Dan quietly adding something to her report. Under "Additional Notes," he'd written: "Hypothesis: Subject is a distant cousin of a Dinosaur, explaining its attraction to human camping activities and processed sugar products."

"I hate you," Sara muttered, fighting back a smile as she deleted his addition.

"No, you hate that I might be right. Imagine the headlines: 'First Martian Life Form Discovered - Loves S'mores.'"

CONCLUSION - MARS: NOT QUITE EARTH, BUT WE'RE TRYING

Sara stood at the viewing dome, gazing out at the vast Martian landscape. The red planet's surface stretched out before her, a tapestry of rust-colored plains, towering volcanoes, and deep canyons. In the distance, a dust devil swirled, a reminder of the planet's ever-present atmospheric quirks.

She chuckled to herself, remembering her first days on Mars. How overwhelmed she'd been by the challenges, the constant threat of death by decompression, the struggle to grow edible food that didn't taste like regret. Now, years later, it all seemed... well, not normal, but a kind of chaotic routine she'd come to embrace.

Her comm panel pinged, and she glanced down to see a colony-announcement:
Attention Martians!

> Today marks the 50th anniversary of our first settlement.
> To celebrate, we're having a colony-party.
> Oxygen rations will be increased by 5% for the duration of the event.
> Remember our motto: Breathe responsibly!"

Sara smiled. Only on Mars would increased oxygen consumption be considered a luxury.

As she made her way to the celebration, she passed by familiar sights that once seemed so alien. The hydroponic gardens, where vegetables grew in defiance of Mars' inhospitable soil. The antigravity gym, where colonists fought a constant battle against muscle atrophy with equipment that looked more like medieval torture devices than exercise machines. The recycling center, known as "Second Chance Station," where every scrap of material was repurposed with an efficiency that would make Earth's environmentalists weep with joy.

The party was in full swing when she arrived. Colonists floated around in the low gravity, sipping on algae-based cocktails that had been named "Red Planet Punch." In one corner, a group was attempting to play low-G volleyball, the ball spending more time arcing through the air than actually being hit.

Dan spotted her and waved her over, nearly spilling his drink in the process. "Sara! Can you believe it? Fifty years! When I signed up for this, I thought I'd last maybe a year before running back to Earth. Now? I can't imagine living anywhere else."
Sara nodded in agreement. "I know what you mean. Remember when we used to complain about the food? Now I actually crave those hydroponic tomatoes that taste like batteries."
"And the dust!" Alex chimed in, joining their conversation. "I used to spend hours trying to keep it out of my living space. Now? I just consider it free insulation."

They all laughed, sharing stories of their early days on Mars. The time the entire colony had to evacuate because someone had set the atmospheric regulator to "Venus" instead of "Mars." The great coffee shortage of '47, which had almost sparked a revolution until someone discovered that roasted Martian lichen made a adequate substitute. The first Martian-born baby, who had taken her first steps in low gravity and floated to the ceiling, much to her parents' mix of pride and panic.

As the night wore on, the colony administrator called for attention.
"My fellow Martians," she began, her voice filled with pride, "fifty years ago, we came to this red planet as explorers, scientists, and dreamers. We faced challenges that would have broken lesser spirits. Dust storms that lasted months, equipment failures that threatened our very existence, and let's not forget the Great Potato Debacle of '39."

A collective groan rose from the crowd at the mention of the infamous incident where an overzealous geneticist had created a strain of potatoes that grew to the size of small cars but tasted like old socks.
"But look at us now," the administrator continued. "We've built a thriving community on a planet that once seemed impossible to inhabit. We've made scientific discoveries that have revolutionized our understanding of the universe. And most importantly, we've created a home."

The party continued well into the Martian night. Groups of colonists huddled together, sharing stories and laughter that echoed through the dome's curved walls.

"Hey, have you heard the latest Martian joke?" Chen asked, his eyes twinkling with mischief. The group around him leaned in closer, knowing his reputation for collecting the colony's best humor.

"So, a terraformer walks into the hydroponics lab," Chen began, barely containing his grin. "He sees this potato plant that's grown through the ceiling, right? The botanist is just standing there, staring up at it. The terraformer asks, 'What's wrong?' And the botanist says, 'I think I made a mistake with the gravity settings.' The terraformer looks at the plant, looks at the botanist, and says, 'Well, I guess that's what they call a spud-nik!'"

The group erupted in groans and chuckles. Only on Mars could a joke combining Soviet space history.

***

Sara glanced around at her fellow colonists, noticing the pride and camaraderie reflected in their expressions. They were a motley crew of scientists, engineers, farmers, and dreamers, all united by their shared experience of turning this harsh, unforgiving planet into a place they could call home.

Sure, life on Mars wasn't perfect. The constant battle against radiation, the never-ending dust, the challenges of growing food and maintaining a breathable atmosphere – these were all part of daily life. But they had adapted, innovated, and even found humor in their struggles.

As the party wound down, Sara found herself back at the viewing dome, looking out at the Martian night sky. The stars seemed brighter here, unobscured by atmospheric pollution. In the distance, Earth shone as a bright blue dot, a reminder of where they had come from but no longer a place they yearned to return to.

A popular saying among the colonists floated through her mind: "Mars – it's not perfect, but at least the traffic's lighter than Earth... most days." She chuckled, remembering the last dust storm that had turned the Central thoroughfare into an impromptu ski slope.

Life on here was challenging, often absurd, and some times terrifying. But it was also exhilarating, filled with discovery, and united by a sense of purpose that was hard to find anywhere else in the solar system.

As she turned to head back to her quarters, Sara took one last look at the red landscape. "Happy anniversary," she whispered. "Here's to another fifty years of dust, danger, and some of the best damn hydroponic tomatoes in the galaxy."

With a smile on her face and a spring in her low-gravity step, Sara headed home. Tomorrow would bring new challenges, new absurdities, and new opportunities for discovery. But that was life now – Never boring, rarely safe, always red, and somehow home

After all, they weren't just surviving on Mars anymore. They were thriving, one dust-covered, low-gravity, oxygen-rationed day at a time.